D1375021

Text copyright © Belinda Hollyer 2002
Illustrations copyright © David Kearney 2002
Book copyright © Hodder Wayland 2002

Consultant: Kimberley Reynolds, University of Surrey, Roehampton
Editor: Katie Orchard

Published in Great Britain in 2002
by Hodder Wayland, an imprint of
Hodder Children's Books

Cataloguing in Publication Data
Hollyer, Belinda
Jane Eyre. – (Classic Collection)
1. Governesses – England – Juvenile fiction 2. England –
Social life and customs – 19th century – Juvenile fiction
3. Children's stories
I. Title II. Brontë, Charlotte, 1816–1855
823.9'14 [J]

ISBN 0 7502 3669 8

Printed and bound in Hong Kong

Hodder Children's Books
A division of Hodder Headline Limited
338 Euston Road, London NW1 3BH

The Classic Collection

Charlotte Brontë's

Jane Eyre

Retold by Belinda Hollyer
Illustrated by David Kearney

an imprint of Hodder Children's Books

An artist's impression of Charlotte Brontë,
1816–1855.

Introduction to Charlotte Brontë

Charlotte Brontë was the daughter of a clergyman, and was born in Yorkshire in 1816. Her two elder sisters died in childhood and her mother died when Charlotte was six. Charlotte was left in charge of her two younger sisters, Anne and Emily, and her brother, Branwell. The Brontë's surroundings were bleak and harsh but the children created their own amusements, and invented two imaginary kingdoms based on a box of wooden soldiers. The 'kingdom of Angria' was ruled over by Charlotte and Branwell; the 'kingdom of Gondal' was ruled over by Anne and Emily. The children also produced their own tiny magazines, imitating the important journals of the time. All of the Brontë children later became writers.

Like her heroine, Jane Eyre, Charlotte worked as a governess for a time, but she longed to write novels. Very few women could become successful writers in nineteenth-century England, and so when *Jane Eyre* was first published in 1847 the author's name was given as 'Currer Bell', to make her sound like a man.

The story of a penniless orphan girl whose courageous spirit triumphs over cruelty and tragedy was an immediate success. Jane's humour, intelligence and instinctive goodness attract Mr Rochester, and make her a lively character – but when the book was first published, Jane's rebellion against injustice and misfortune was thought shocking.

Charlotte wrote three other novels – *The Professor*, *Shirley* and *Villette*, but none was as successful as *Jane Eyre*. Charlotte's life was surrounded by tragedy, for Emily, Anne and Branwell all died before her, and she herself died when she was only thirty-nine, just a few months after she had married.

This shortened version of *Jane Eyre* only tells the bare outline of the story; the orginal version is much longer. If you enjoy reading this story and want to discover more of what happened to Jane, try reading the original novel.

A New Life

As the horse-cab rocked through the night on my journey to Thornfield Hall, I stared out of the window into the misty dark. A hundred doubts and excitements filled my mind.

Eight years had passed since the day I had been taken to Lowood School as a penniless orphan – sent there by my Aunt Reed. How frightened I had been! How I had hated Aunt Reed and her cruelty to me. Not a scrap of affection had been shown to me by her or her three children, and I had been glad to escape from them.

But Lowood School had been harsh and cruel, too, and I had suffered dreadfully there, as all the pupils had. We were cold and hungry – hungry enough to eat the burnt porridge and rancid meat we were served. Semi-starvation and a harsh, unfeeling discipline were the rule at Lowood. Only after an outbreak of typhus fever had killed many of the pupils, including my own dearest friend, Helen Burns, did conditions improve.

Now I was eighteen, and I had been a teacher at Lowood, instead of a pupil, for the past two years. The school had become a kinder place, and I had been content. But I was also impatient to see the world, so I had advertised for a job as a governess. And here I was – on my way to Thornfield Hall, to look after a little girl in the care of a Mrs Fairfax.

But what if Mrs Fairfax turned out to be as severe as Mr Brocklehurst, the director of Lowood, had been? Or as grim and unpleasant as my Aunt Reed had been to me? What if…?

"Here's Thornfield Hall now, Miss Eyre," said the driver, breaking in on my thoughts.

We clattered up a long drive to a large house.
Candlelight gleamed from one window, although
the rest were dark.

I took a deep breath, and stepped from the
horse-cab into my new life.

At first, Thornfield Hall was better than I had
dared to hope. Mrs Fairfax was kind and
motherly, my room was pretty, and the house
was elegant with lovely grounds. Even little
Adèle, my pupil, seemed sweet and good-natured.

But there was one mystery – the owner of Thornfield Hall.

"Are you not the owner, Mrs Fairfax?" I had asked on my first night.

"Why, bless you my dear, no – I'm only the housekeeper!" she laughed. "Mr Edward Rochester owns Thornfield, and Adèle is his ward. But Mr Rochester is not here – he often goes away for months at a time. I don't know when we will see him again."

I was curious to meet this Mr Rochester, but soon another mystery puzzled me. When Mrs Fairfax showed me around the house I heard a terrifying sound in the attics – a moaning laugh that started low, and ended in a shriek that echoed through the rooms.

"What on earth is that?" I asked Mrs Fairfax in alarm.

"It's just Grace Poole, one of the servants," she answered, dismissing my fears. Then she called through the attics to a door at the end, "Grace! Too much noise – remember your orders!"

The door opened and a servant appeared, curtsied silently, and returned to the room. She looked so ordinary – how odd that her laugh was so ghostly.

I tried to dismiss the incident from my mind as I gave Adèle her lessons, and walked in the gardens. But that moaning laughter I had heard troubled me. What sort of servant was Grace Poole? And where was Mr Rochester? Would he ever come back to Thornfield?

The Dark Rider

Months passed quietly, and I grew restless. Now and then I mounted the stairs to the attics, and climbed out on to the roof to look out across the hills, wondering what life was like in other places. Sometimes when I was there I heard Grace Poole's strange laugh, and shivered at the sound. Yet I grew fond of Adèle, and worked hard with her.

One winter afternoon I walked to the nearest village to post a letter for Mrs Fairfax. It was cold and growing dark, but I sat on a stile to enjoy the view before walking on to the village. It was then I heard a horse on the road behind me, travelling fast. Another moment and the clattering hooves had swept around the corner, and a horse and rider thundered past, with a huge dog running behind them.

But then the horse slipped on the icy road, and with a scramble of hooves and a cry from the rider it was down!

"Are you injured, sir?" I asked, jumping from the stile. The man looked stern and I was nervous, but determined to help if I could.

"Stand to one side!" he replied as he struggled up, and then encouraged the horse to its feet again. The horse was unhurt, but when the man tried to walk it was clear that his ankle was badly sprained.

As I attempted to help the man to mount the horse, he seemed curious about me. He asked me who I was and where I lived, still wearing a stern and unfriendly expression. I answered him briefly.

Then with a sudden call of, "Come, Pilot!" to the dog, the man and his horse wheeled around and disappeared into the night as swiftly as they had arrived.

My adventure – such as it was – was over, and I delivered the letter and returned to Thornfield as quickly as I could.

But when I entered there was a dog in the hall – surely the same one I had met earlier with the fallen rider?

"Pilot!" I called softly, and the dog wagged his tail and padded across to me.

"Whose dog is this?" I asked one of the servants.

"He came with the master," was the reply. "With Mr Rochester. We've sent for the surgeon – Mr Rochester's horse fell on the road from Hay, and his ankle is sprained."

So it was Mr Rochester, my employer, whom I had met in the lane – that dark and frowning rider!

Fire in the Night

The following evening Adèle and I took tea with Mr Rochester. Adèle played with Pilot while the master of the house questioned me. He still seemed stern and his manner abrupt, but I liked his forthright way and I found him easy to talk to. I had no experience of society manners, and polite conversation would have bewildered me. His straightforward style suited me very well.

As the weeks passed, I grew to like Mr Rochester more and more. He was not really handsome – and yet his strong face and confident manner appealed to me. He often seemed proud and harsh – and yet to me he was kind and encouraging. His coldness melted away when we spoke, and I dared to think that he enjoyed my company.

I still knew little about him, but I sensed that he was deeply troubled by something in his past – perhaps some old mistake that still tormented him. When I asked Mrs Fairfax about him she turned my questions away. What could his secret be?

Mr Rochester had been back at Thornfield for eight weeks when I woke suddenly one night. Something had disturbed me. There it was again – a sort of murmuring groan. And then something – or *someone* – outside in the gallery brushed across my door.

I sat up in bed, chilled with fear. "Who's there?" I called.

Then came a demonic laugh that faded to a sort of gurgling moan.

I threw back the covers and hurried into my clothes – I would run to Mrs Fairfax for help. But when I peered out of my door into the gallery I saw no one. Then I suddenly noticed smoke – smoke that billowed from Mr Rochester's room!

My fears forgotten, I flew to help. The bed curtains were ablaze, and Mr Rochester was fast asleep. I snatched his jug and basin of water and threw the water on to the flames. The fire continued! Back to my own room for my water jug: back again to his room with it.

There! The flames were out – and Mr Rochester lay in the middle of his soaked bedclothes peering up at me.

"Miss Eyre?" he asked, bewildered. "Is there a flood?"

"No, sir, but there has been a fire," I replied.
I fetched a candle so we could see better, and
explained what I had heard and found.

He looked grave. "Wait here for me. Do
nothing until I come back," he instructed and
vanished upstairs.

He returned, pale and concerned, and took my hand in both his own. "Thank you, Miss Eyre – Jane. You have saved my life," he said. "I knew when we met that you would do me good in some way. But for now I can say no more." And he swore me to secrecy – not even Mrs Fairfax was to know what had happened.

How strange this was! That laugh I'd heard belonged to Grace Poole. It *must* have something to do with her – but what?

Company at Thornfield

The next morning I thought only of seeing
Mr Rochester again, but to my dismay I learned
he had left early, to stay with friends. I knew it
was impossible that there could be anything
between us – I was only the plain little governess.
And yet – the way he had looked at me when he
had taken my hand and thanked me…

"Stop!" I told myself. "This is foolishness."

And foolishness it clearly was, for Mrs Fairfax explained that some of Mr Rochester's friends were coming to stay, including a beautiful woman whom Mr Rochester admired.

My heart ached, but I forced myself to be sensible. And when Mr Rochester returned with his friends and I saw how lovely Blanche Ingram was, I knew that I could never compete.

One night, when Mr Rochester's friends were
still visiting, a Mr Mason arrived to see him on
business, joined his friends for dinner, and
stayed the night. That night, Thornfield was
woken by a shriek of pain from the attics!

"Help! Help! Help!" – desperate shouts rang
through the house.

Everyone rushed from their rooms to see what
was wrong, all calling for candles and crying out
in alarm.

Mr Rochester appeared calmly from the attic staircase. A servant had had a nightmare, he explained. There was nothing to worry about.

I watched him soothe his guests back to bed, but I knew that he was lying. Something was terribly wrong, and I felt certain that he would need me.

When he tapped on my door I followed him through the dark house, and climbed with him to the attics.

And – there was Mr Mason, half-fainting, with blood pouring from one arm and murmuring a phrase that chilled me to the bone.

"She bit me!"

She? It must be Grace Poole! Why did Mr Rochester keep such a servant? What was her hold over him?

I sat alone with Mr Mason while Mr Rochester rode to fetch a doctor. I shuddered with fear that Grace Poole would burst in at any moment. But whatever I could do to help, I would.

Hours later Mr Rochester returned with a doctor, who bound Mr Mason's wounds and took him away.

Dawn was approaching as we watched the carriage depart. It had been the strangest night of my life, but I did not question Mr Rochester about his secret. I only made him promise that he would be careful, and he swore that Grace Poole would do no more harm.

I wished he could love me as I now knew I loved him – but Blanche Ingram was the one he would marry. At least he saw me as his friend – at least I had helped him.

Unexpected News

The next day unexpected news came. My Aunt Reed was dying, and had asked for me. I had hoped never to see her again, but I knew that I must go. Old unhappy times crowded back into my mind, but I tried to be kind to Aunt Reed, and I stayed with her until she died.

And then I returned to Thornfield.

I had longed to see Mr Rochester again, but when I did I was overwhelmed with emotion. In spite of myself, I longed for his love.

The next two weeks were the happiest I had ever spent. The summer was glorious! Mr Rochester was at home, and there was no more talk of Miss Ingram. And then one evening he told me that he wanted to marry – *me*. I could scarcely believe it. It was like a dream… He loved *me*, Jane Eyre! Blanche Ingram was nothing to him.

The next month was a whirlwind of wedding plans and excitement.

But on the eve of our wedding, I woke in the night to a dazzle of candlelight in my eyes.

Someone was in my room.

The Nightmare

A tall woman stood at my mirror with her back to me. She threw my wedding veil over her own head and as she turned I caught sight of her face – a savage, terrifying face – like a vampire! She ripped my veil and trampled it. And then she moved silently towards me, holding up the candle.

I fainted with fear.

It was dawn when I woke again, and the woman had vanished.

Mr Rochester – Edward – persuaded me that it had been a dream, or that Grace Poole had ripped my veil. So I put it aside, and used a plain square of silk instead.

Edward seemed determined that nothing should stop our marriage. We hurried to the church without delay. He took my hand and we prepared to make our vows.

But then a voice called from the back of the church.

"This marriage cannot continue! Mr Rochester has a wife still living! She is my sister!"

Chilled with dread, I turned – and saw Mr Mason.

My husband-to-be said nothing. He led us all
back to Thornfield, and up to the attics. There
behind a locked door was Grace Poole – but
there, too, was something grovelling on all fours
and growling like an animal. It gave a terrible
cry. It stood up and bellowed. It was the woman
from my nightmare!

She sprang forward with a shriek and attacked Mr Rochester – she even managed to rip open his cheek before he could pin her arms down.

Grace gave him a rope and he bound the poor demented creature to a chair. Then Mr Rochester turned defiantly to the horrified guests.

"Yes, I am married," he said bitterly. "*This* is my wife! Compare her with Jane, and judge me if you dare. Now leave – I must shut up my prize."

A Voice From the Past

The awful secret was revealed at last. I did not judge Edward Rochester – I loved him still – but he had done wrong, and as long as his wife lived I could not stay. Grief-stricken, I ran away the next morning.

With neither money nor friends to help me I turned to begging, and almost died on the road. But a kind family took me in, and despite the fact that I could not – would not – tell them of my past, they trusted me. I taught at their village school.

A whole year passed. Slowly, I began to gain some peace of mind, although Mr Rochester and my life at Thornfield were never far from my thoughts.

But one evening I suddenly heard Mr Rochester calling to me out of nowhere – his

own beloved voice.

"Jane! Jane! Jane!"

"Wait for me! Oh, I will come!" I replied, running outside. "Where are you?"

The voice faded, but I knew I must go to him. I travelled back to Thornfield immediately.

A dreadful sight awaited me. The house was a
fire-blackened ruin, with the silence of death
about it. Was I too late? Would I never see
Edward Rochester again – was he dead?

I found out what had happened from the local
innkeeper. Mr Rochester's wife had started
another fire that had burned down the house,
and he had been injured trying to save her. The
poor woman had died, and Edward Rochester
now lived quietly nearby – with one hand lost,
and his sight gone.

I drove to see him immediately, and found him – so changed, yet still the man I loved.

My heart ached for that proud man, now caged in by blindness. His pride had burned away with fire and grief, but he loved me still.

Reader, I married him. I am blessed to live with the one I love best in the world. God has been kind, my dear Edward has partly recovered his sight, and I am happier than I ever thought possible when I journeyed to Thornfield Hall and a new life.

The Classic Collection

Look out for these other titles in *The Classic Collection*:

A Christmas Carol Retold by Tony Bradman
This is Dickens' classic tale of the miserly Scrooge who is
visited by three ghostly figures. Will he change his cold-hearted
ways forever as a result, or die a miserable old man? A dramatic
retelling of this unforgettable Christmas story.

Gulliver's Travels Retold by Beverley Birch
Gulliver is shipwrecked and washed ashore on the exotic island
of Lilliput – where the people are only six inches tall! This is
just the start of Gulliver's unbelievable adventure. A thrilling
retelling of one of the most exciting fantasy stories ever written.

The Pardoner's Tale Retold by Jan Dean
On a trip to Canterbury, the crooked Pardoner tells a crooked
story about a gang of youths who decide to hunt down Death
and kill him. Little do they know that Death will find them
first! A lively retelling of a story that is as hilarious today as
when it was written over six centuries ago.

You can buy all these books from your local bookseller, or
order them direct from the publisher. For more information
about *The Classic Collection*, write to: *The Sales Department,
Hodder Children's Books, a division of Hodder Headline Limited,
338 Euston Road, London NW1 3BH.*